The Cow That Laid an Egg

HarperCollins *Children's Books*

by Andy Cutbill

illustrated by Russell Ayto

Marjorie the cow felt
down in the dumps.
"What's wrong, Marge?"
clucked the chickens.

"I don't feel special," said Marjorie. "I can't ride bicycles and do handstands like the other cows. I just feel so ordinary."

The following morning
there was an almighty commotion
in the barnyard.

"I've laid
an egg!"

shrieked Marjorie.

All the other cows
were astonished.
None of them had ever
laid an egg before.

Even the farmer came running.
"Oh, my goodness!" he cried.
"Marjorie's laid an egg!"

The farmer's
wife called the
local newspaper.

People came
from far and wide.

"We're extremely proud of Marjorie," announced the farmer to the crowd.

Marjorie felt much
more special now.
And the chickens were
as pleased as Punch too.

But the other cows weren't so happy.

"We don't think you
laid that egg,"
the cows said to Marjorie.
"We think the crafty
chickens did it."

Marjorie felt shocked.

"prove it,"

said the chickens.

So they all waited for the egg to hatch. Day after day they watched, as Marjorie sat on the egg to keep it warm. But nothing happened.

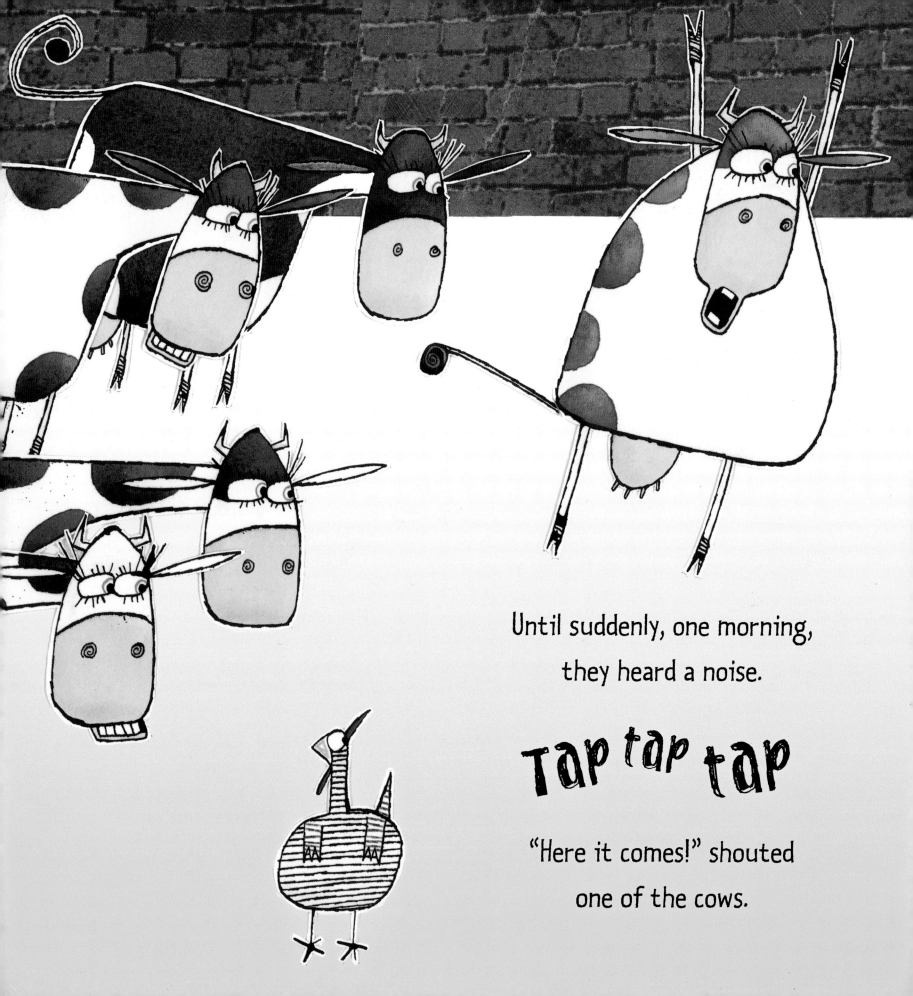

Until suddenly, one morning,
they heard a noise.

Tap tap tap

"Here it comes!" shouted
one of the cows.

And as Marjorie
stood up...

tap **tap** tap

the egg

cracked

open

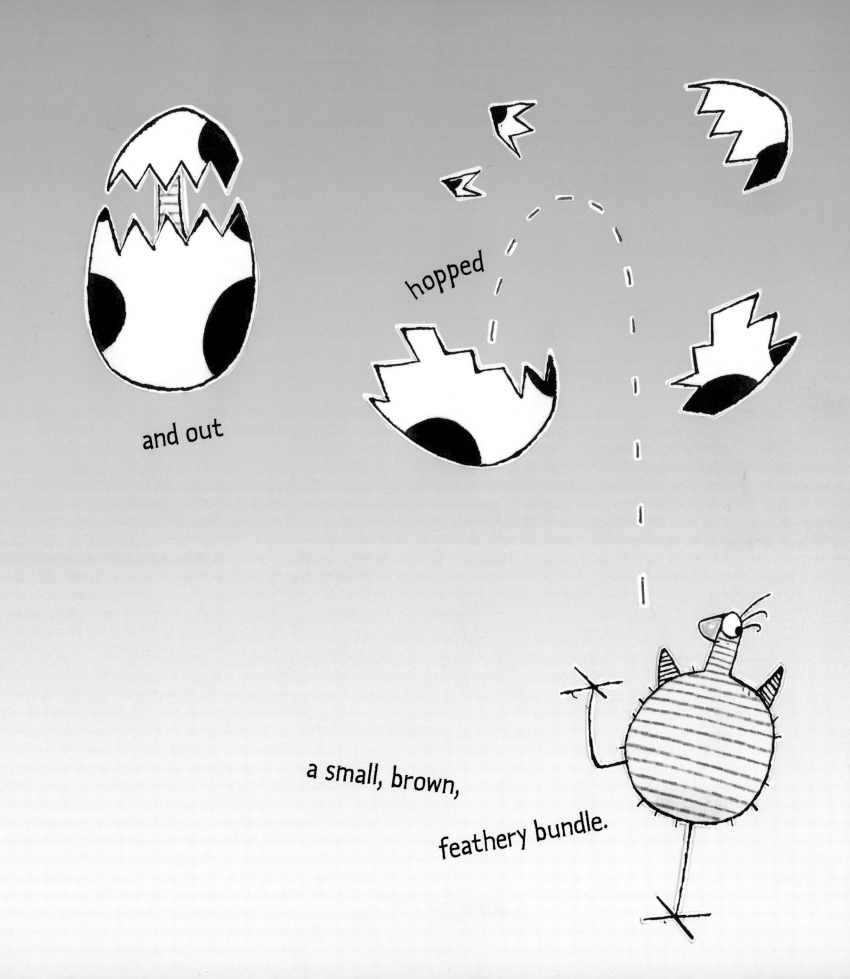

and out

hopped

a small, brown,

feathery bundle.

"There," said one of the cows, nodding. "A Chicken!"

Suddenly, the tiny creature looked up at Marjorie.

OOOOOO!"

it said loudly.

Marjorie smiled and held her baby tight.
"A cow," she said.

And she promptly named it Daisy.